the water

the sun

the earth

the tree

Delphine Durand

B O B & C⁰.

the sky

the emptiness

God

and Bob

Tate Publishing

On the blank page

there's a vast EMPTINESS

all alone.

Everyone is late.

The sky is still in the shower

and the earth is doing its hair,

and the water, who is in the clouds

and in the shower at the same time, is forced to wait too.

And the EMPTINESS taps its foot impatiently.

And the story waits;

the story would like to begin . . .

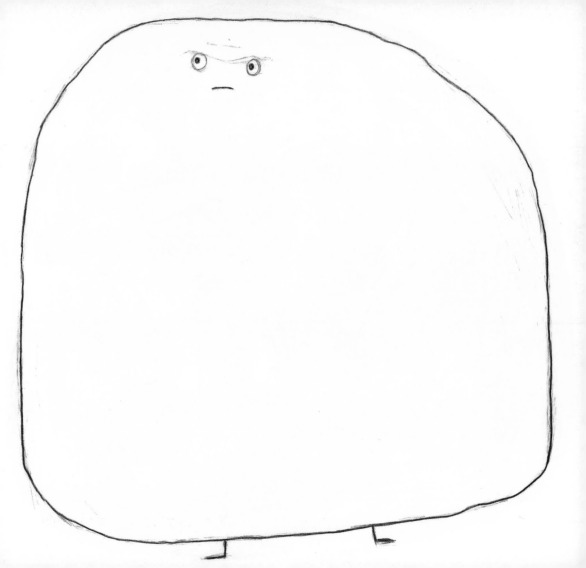

The water, who is fed up waiting,

takes its clouds and leaves the shower

and starts to settle in.

It spills out all over the place and tickles the EMPTINESS.

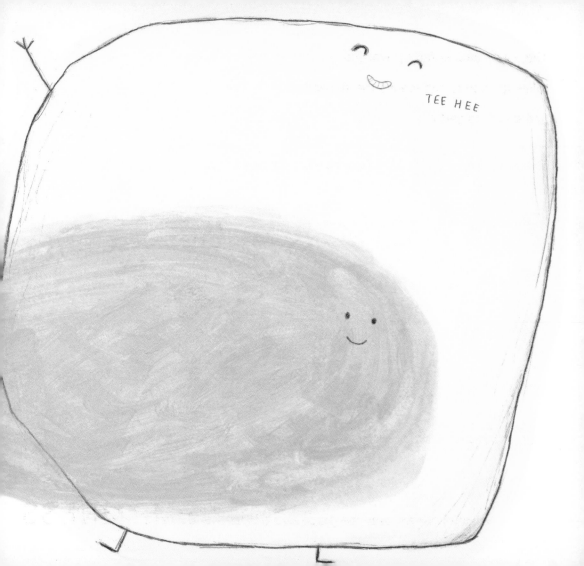

TEE HEE

BoB arrives, as expected, on page 13.

But all of a sudden he is underwater,

and that was not expected.

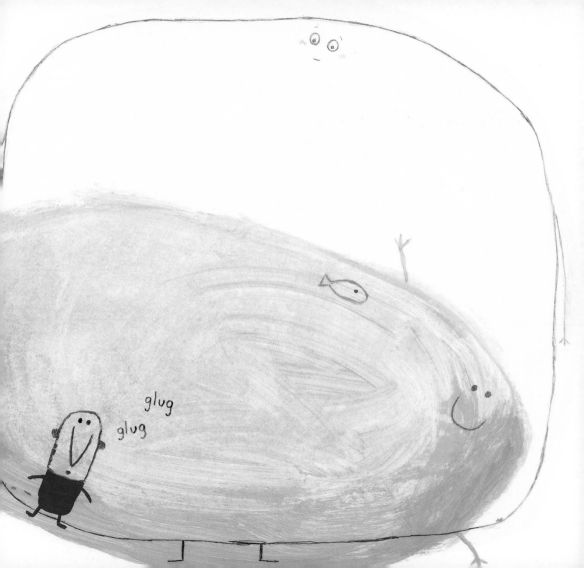

glug
glug

Move along, water! says the earth, who arrives at last.

Not a moment too soon, says BoB;

I nearly swallowed a mouthful.

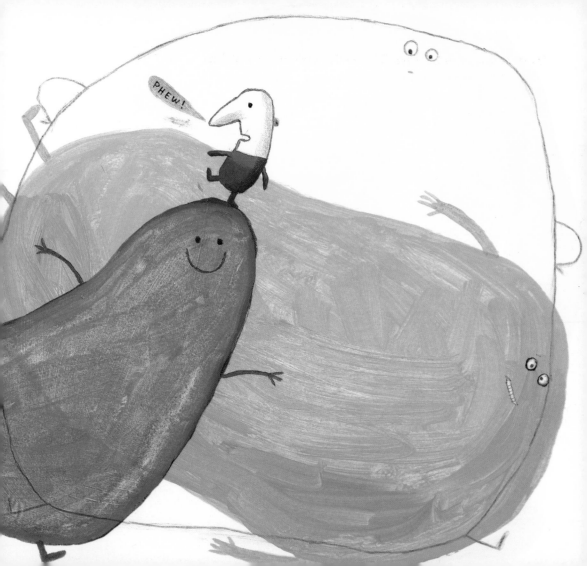

Now look! The wheat field's waterlogged, says the earth,

whose *hair's* all wet.

If only you'd get here on time, says BoB.

The sky arrives at last . . .

earth   sky   water

OK, I'd better be off now, says the EMPTINESS

(who is finally full).

What are we going to do now? asks BoB.

All we have to do is start, says the sky. I'm ready if you are.

But you haven't even any clouds, says the water.

You just need to evaporate and then there'll be some, says the earth to the water.

But where's the sun? asks BoB.

Uh oh! says the sky. I've gone and left it on the bath mat!

Just great! says the water.

Just great! says the earth.

Just great! says BoB.

Who left the sun in the bathroom again?! asks the EMPTINESS,

who's back again.

Put it there! says BoB.

And now you'll have to go somewhere else, says the sky. It's full here.

Yeah! says the fullness.

Yeah!

Harrumph . . . says the EMPTINESS as it departs.

I missed the start, says the sun.

Don't worry! We haven't even got there yet, says the earth.

Where are we then? asks BoB.

In the beginning . . . says the water.

So let's begin! says the sky.

Where's the story? asks the water.

Here I am , says the story.

Go ahead then, says BoB.

That's what I'm doing , says the story.

What? Is that it? asks the earth, asks the water, asks BoB.

NO NO IT ISN'T OVER , says the story.

THAT'S ONLY THE START...

Ha! So here we are! says BoB.

Where? asks the earth.

At the start! says the fullness.

I don't understand a thing, says the EMPTINESS

(who's been listening at the door).

OK, says the earth. I have some complaints!

The water's taking up all the space!

That's nothing to do with me, says the story;
I'm only in charge of the ideas.

I have an idea! says B o B. What if we grow a tree?

Alright, says the earth.

Alright, says the water.

Alright, says the sky.

Alright, says the sun.

And me? What do I do? asks BoB.

You? You watch the tree grow, says the story.

That's quite a story! says the water.

Not bad, eh? says the sky.

You think it's easy making a tree grow! says the earth.

Here, let me help, says the water. Just tell me when.

So in the end I don't get to do anything in this story! says BoB.

BoB thinks things over . . .

I think I'm God! says BoB.

Nope! I'm God! says **GOD** (who was passing by).

Bother! says BoB.

This story's taking a strange turn, says the earth.

OK. I'll leave you to it, says **GOD**. I haven't had my shower yet.

He's terribly late, says the sky.

He's got it easy, says the water.

That wasn't even God; it was a trickster from another world, says the earth.

It came as a surprise to me too . . . says the sun.

Now what? asks BoB.

I don't know, says the story.

I think I've lost all my ideas ...

Who's left their ideas all over the bath mat again?!

asks the EMPTINESS, who has arrived back, sounding a bit irritated.

Uh... says the story.

They're ruined, says BoB. They've been squashed flat by everyone's feet!

What are you talking about? asks the tree (who has started to grow).

Anyway, it's too late, says the fullness.

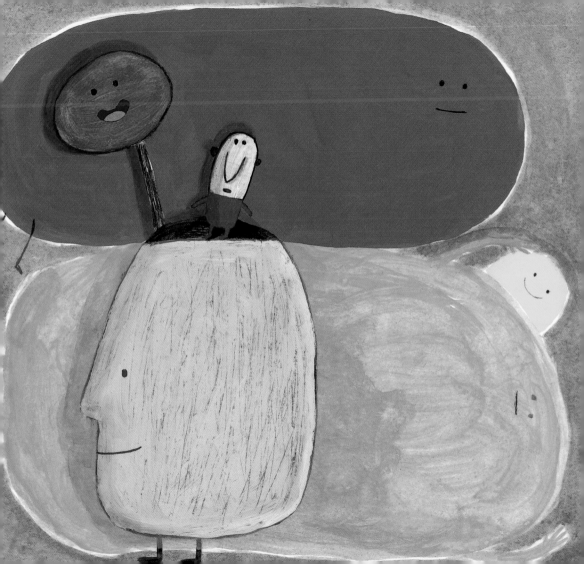

Too late for what? asks BoB.

To remake the world, says the earth.

I suppose so, says BoB. Besides, I'm sleepy.

Good night, says the sun.

Good night, says the earth.

Good night, says the water.

Good night, says BoB.

But I'm not sleepy, says the tree.

Good day, says the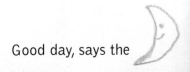

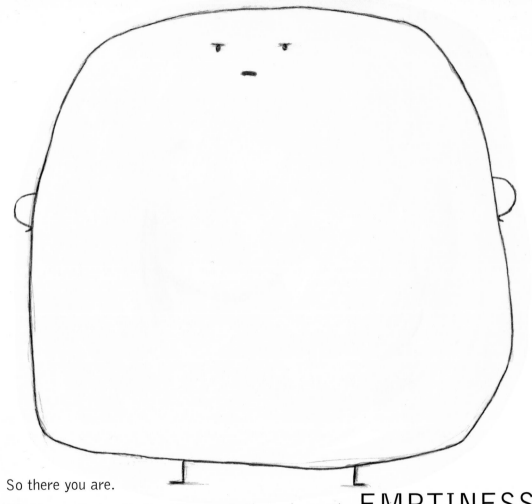

So there you are.

It's always the same. I'm all alone in the end, says the EMPTINESS.